# THE PRESIDENT WHO DIDN'T READ
### BY J.E. TURNER

Copyright © 2020 by Jahid Turner and Darnell Wynn

All Rights Reserved.
Published in the United States of America by Turner Wynn Publications.
Library of Congress Cataloging-in-Publication Data available upon request.

Manufactured in the United States of America

Second Edition
Edited by Keiana Smith

Disclaimer: This is a work of fiction. Names, characters, businesses, places, events, locales, and incidents are either the products of the author's imagination or used in a fictitious manner. Any resemblance to actual persons, living or dead, or actual events is purely coincidental.

There once was a president who won his votes with gold.

The job he won was not much fun,
which he was never told.

He had to read...

He tried, at first, to pay someone to read his daily briefs.

"They can read, so I can lead and watch my ratings leap!"

But the man he paid
was too afraid
to offer any blues.

So, things got bad and crowds grew mad of the ignorance that ensued.

The president set out to solve this blunder
with what he thought was smart.

He fired the guy he hired,
and got a chum to play the part.

The next guy he paid soon grew afraid
of the tantrums the president threw.

So, he stopped the bother and called his father, for he knew he was a goner too.

The president fired another reader.

20

And another...
and another.

He howled and spit, he cursed and ripped,
but his ratings did not recover.

One day, the first lady suggested,
"Maybe you should do it yourself."

The president replied,
"So silly, you tried!"

"I'll read for myself."

He skimmed and he flipped,

then hurried to make birdies and chips forgetting the people in need.

He tweeted and trolled
and lost all control.

He did everything he wanted, except read.

The nation grew louder as lives turned to powder, and the president just golfed away.

In the end he learned a lesson earned,
and one that we all should teach.

Read the rules or be the fool
who winds up getting impeached.

Made in the USA
Middletown, DE
06 December 2020